It's Silly Time

Written By: **Kim Mitzo Thompson, Karen Mitzo Hilderbrand**
Executive Producers: **Kim Mitzo Thompson, Karen Mitzo Hilderbrand**
Music Arranged By: **Hal Wright**
Music Vocals: **The Nashville Kids Sound**
Illustrated By: **Sharon Lane Holm**
Book Design: **Jennifer Birchler**

Published By:
Twin Sisters Productions
4710 Hudson Drive
Stow, OH 44224 USA
www.twinsisters.com   1-800-248-8946

©℗2010 Twin Sisters IP, LLC
All Rights Reserved. Made in China.

Read- and Sing-Along is a registered
trademark of Twin Sisters IP, LLC.

ISBN-13: 978-159922-508-1

It's not time to be quiet. No, not at all.

It's not time to be still. Let's have a ball.

It's not time to relax or sit and wait.

For it's time to be silly and that's what I want to be!

Because it's *silly*, *silly*, *silly*, *silly*, *silly*, *silly* time.
I'm feeling all giggly-wiggly, funny, and fine.

It's fun to be silly. That's what I want to do—
be silly, silly, silly. Won't you be silly, too?

It's not time to rest in a quiet place.

It's not time for bed. Come on, let's race!

It's not time to whisper or go to sleep.

For it's time to be **silly** and that's what I want to be!

Because it's silly, silly, silly, silly, silly, silly time.

I'm feeling all giggly-wiggly, funny, and fine.

It's fun to be silly. That's what I want to do—
be silly, silly, silly. Won't you be silly, too?

Because it's silly, silly, silly, silly, silly, silly time.

I'm feeling all giggly-wiggly, funny, and fine.

It's fun to be silly. That's what I want to do—
be silly, silly, silly. Won't you be silly, too?

It's **silly, silly, silly** time! Together with your child…

Hop like a kangaroo!

Waddle like a duck!

Flap like a bird!

Slither like a snake!

Crawl like a crab!

…Can you think of other silly actions?